Rupert and the Star Girl

EGMONT

Rupert and Bill are at the treehouse, looking through the telescope. Rupert closes one eye and looks with the other. He sees something very bright tumbling through the sky.

"Come and see, Bill – QUICK!" calls Rupert. Bill looks through the telescope and sees a shimmering glow that vanishes into the woods.

"Let's go find it," says Rupert, grabbing Bill by the arm as they run down the treehouse.

3

Rupert and Bill hurry through the woods, and hear someone crying. They run towards the sobbing sounds and find a little Star Girl sitting on the ground. She has a soft, twinkling aura around her.

"She's a star!" whispers Bill in amazement.

"Hello. Are you all right?" asks Rupert.

"I . . . I . . . think so," she replies and wipes her tears. "Hello. I'm Astra."

"I'm Rupert and this is Bill," says Rupert.

"What are you doing here?" wonders Bill.

"I've always wanted to know what the Earth was like. So this morning when all the other stars were going to sleep, I crept away to have a closer look. But I slipped and tumbled out of the sky!" Astra giggles at her own silly mistake.

They all decide to play hide-and-seek, and Rupert starts counting while the other two hide.

Deep in the woods, Raggety the tree elf is practising his woodland magic on a purple flower to help it grow. He tries several spells but nothing happens. "Raggety magic not working!" he says, and tries his spell again . . .

"Sunbeams come. Warm and bright.
Woods are dark. Plants need light!"

Slowly, a thin sunbeam shines through the trees and the flower blooms beautifully. "Whoo-hoo! Raggety done it!" leaps Raggety.

While trying to find a place to hide, Astra meets Raggety. He is startled by her twinkling glow and can't speak. "Hello! I'm Astra. Who are you?" she asks. "I saw you magic that sunbeam. You're clever!"

"Yes . . . please . . . thank you. Raggety!" he says, his cheeks blushing a little.

Astra spies Rupert and Bill walking towards her. She steps into Raggety's sunbeam and is almost invisible. "Don't tell them you've seen me," she says, quietly.

"**H**ello Raggety! Have you seen Astra?" asks Bill. Raggety tries to control his giggles, "No, no . . . sorry . . . thank you!"

Rupert and Bill search everywhere, but they cannot find her. Astra starts giggling, enjoying her trick. "What was that?" says Rupert.

Soon they know the giggles are coming from behind Raggety. In the sunbeam, they find Astra twinkling.

"Found you! Found you!" call Rupert and Bill.

Rupert and Bill invite Astra and Raggety to see their treehouse. Everyone squeals with laughter as they play off the ground tag.

"Can't catch me," teases Astra.

"Oh yes, I can!" says Rupert. He leaps forward to catch her, but Astra shoots up into the air, leaving a trail of sparkle behind her.

"Sizzling stardust!" says Raggety, dazzled.

"**W**hat else can we play?" asks Astra.

"Let's go outside and play football," says Rupert.

Astra had never played football, so Rupert and Bill explain how it works. "You kick the ball . . . like this," shows Rupert, ". . . and you try to get it into the goal here."

Astra takes up her position at the goalpost, excited to play this new earthly game.

"Raggety you're on my team," says Astra.

"Yes . . . please . . . thank you," blushes Raggety. She's the most twinkling girl he has ever seen. Standing next to her, Raggety too has a bright glow.

Rupert and Bill get ready. "High-five," says Rupert, and they clap their hands together. "Let's start!"

Raggety starts the game by dribbling the ball towards the goal. "Nice footwork," says Rupert, impressed.

Bill tackles Raggety, who then loses the ball. "Oops, sorry, not good," says Raggety.

Bill does a fantastic pass to Rupert. "Great pass," shouts Rupert, "and now . . . for a goal . . ." and he shoots the ball towards the goal. The ball whizzes through the air, but Astra leaps up and saves it. As she does so, she leaves another trail of star sparkle behind her.

The sound of giggles and laughter from all four friends fills the woods.

Running around and falling about with laughter, they all get a little tired and think of what to do next.

"Let's play on my scooter," says Rupert. He whizzes across the clearing on his red scooter, weaving speedily through trees and giant mushrooms, and doing wheelies over the bumpy ground.

"Yippee," he calls, as he pulls the handbrake and skids to a halt beside Astra. "Your turn, Astra."

When Astra stands on the scooter, it flies off the ground, showering everyone with colourful sparkles. "How do you do that sparkle thing?" wonders Bill.

"I can give you all shooting star trails if you like," says Astra.

"Yes! Please! Thank you!" the boys say, delightfully.

Astra throws a shower of stardust over them. They all run around, leaving behind sparkling trails and shouting, gleefully.

Soon it begins to get dark and they all return to the treehouse. Astra is very quiet and Raggety sees that she is not twinkling as much as before. "Astra tired?" Raggety tugs at her gently.

"No, but I think I have given away too much of my sparkle! I can't get home without it! And I have to be home before it gets dark. What am I going to do?" says Astra, tearfully.

"Woodland magic might help Astra," says Raggety. "Let's go to the clearing."

Raggety waggles his ears, and leaves and flowers lift up from the ground and shower around him. He blows a puff of wind into the air and says . . .

"Moonbeams come silver bright.
You take Astra home tonight!"

"Thank you, Raggety," says Astra. "Goodbye, Rupert. Goodbye, Bill. Thank you for playing with me."

A silver moonbeam streams through the trees on to Astra, and carries her up and away.

"Raggety miss Astra," says Raggety, sadly.

"How will we know which star is you?" calls Bill.

"I'll twinkle extra brightly at you," replies Astra. The moonbeam fades away and Astra disappears.

"I can see her! Look!" calls Rupert, suddenly. Raggety and Bill look up to see a star twinkling merrily at them. Seeing Astra cheers up Raggety.

The boys run off home, kicking the football to each other and talking about the day's adventures.

The End

First published in Great Britain in 2007
by Egmont UK Limited
239 Kensington High Street, London W8 6SA

ISBN 978 1 4052 3195 4
3 5 7 9 10 8 6 4 2
Printed in China